Curious McCarthy's
Power of Observation

by Tory Christie   illustrated by Mina Price

PICTURE WINDOW BOOKS
a capstone imprint

Curious McCarthy is published by Picture Window Books,
A Capstone Imprint
1710 Roe Crest Drive
North Mankato, Minnesota 56003
www.mycapstone.com

Cataloging-in-Publication Data is available on the Library of Congress website.
ISBN: 978-1-5158-1646-1 (library binding)
ISBN: 978-1-5158-1650-8 (paperback)
ISBN: 978-1-5158-1654-6 (eBook PDF)

Summary: Curious McCarthy, named after the famous scientist Marie Curie, has
decided to become a scientist herself. Her first hypothesis: That her mischievous
younger brother will get noticed before her proper oldest sister, Charlotte. Using
footnotes filled with funny observations, Curious invites readers to read her
observations about her first days at a new school with an old-fashioned teacher and
her entertaining evenings at home with her six brothers and sisters.

Designer: Ashlee Suker

Printed and bound in the United States of America.
010642R

For Charlotte, Emily, Anne, John Glenn,
Benjamin, and Edison. Especially for
Charlotte. Although this is a work of
fiction, sorry I made you so snotty.

DAD Engineer, vegetable lover, breakfast lover . . . as long as it's slurped down with lots of black coffee.

MOM English professor with a very well-trained nose.

CHARLOTTE (age 13) A very appropriate older sister and excellent napkin folder.

EMILY (age 12) She's weird.

MRS. STICKLER (age 103, I think) The teacher with the perfectly curled hair. You can bet that she does NOT pick her nose – even when no one is looking.

AUNT DOLLY A nurse who believes popsicles cure most diseases.

MR. CORNFORTH Principal of Hilltop Elementary – a school that is nowhere near a hill.

The McCarthys

CURIOUS (age 10) Future scientist – unless I catch a horrible slime disease before I have a chance to grow up.

ANNE (age 11) She can't get through a single week without rolling her eyes.

JOHN GLENN (age 8) Named after an astronaut. He should have been named after a clown.

BENJAMIN (age 5) A kindergartner with strict food-touching rules.

EDISON (age 4) The youngest McCarthy without any food rules. He'd probably eat off the floor if you let him.

MR. GRUMPUS School librarian. He spends time fighting the Big Bad Wolf.

LIN TRAN Fourth grader at Hilltop, likely friend.

ROBIN FINCH Fourth grader at Hilltop, unlikely friend.

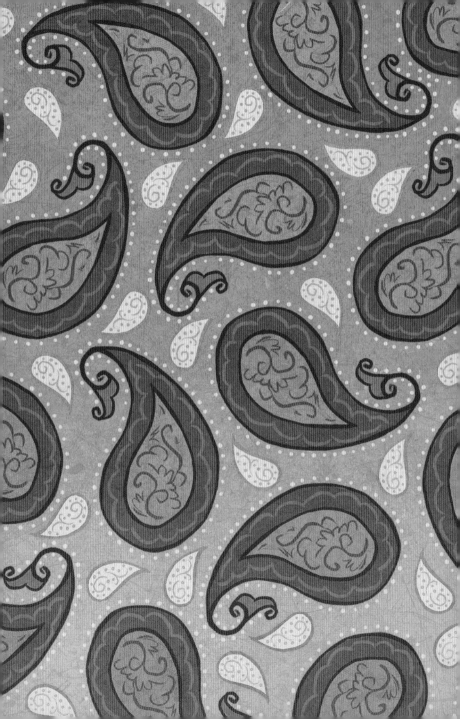

My life began in fourth grade. No, not really. It began on my birthday. But read on and you'll find out why fourth grade made such an impact on my life.

I was going to a new school, even though we didn't move. Our school district had redrawn boundary lines. I should say they hired experts to redraw boundary lines. This means they took out a map and drew lines around groups of houses.

These *experts* had me going to a new school across town. All of my friends stayed at our old school. I think my four-year-old brother Edison could have drawn better boundaries. He's pretty good with a crayon.

I would start my fourth-grade year at Hilltop Elementary. And it wasn't even at the top of a hill. How did this school come to be called Hilltop?

That was just one of the questions that I would ponder as a fourth grader.

My name is Curious McCarthy. I am a scientist. I haven't always been a scientist. I have been a scientist for exactly six days, nineteen hours, and thirteen minutes. My first week as a scientist began something like this . . .

Monday, 8:04 a.m.

It was my second week at this new school. My teacher Mrs. Stickler announced it was Fiction Week. And Fiction Week didn't start out so great. Mrs. Stickler moved me to the lowest reading group — the Green Group. This is not good when your mother teaches English.

Or when your three older sisters are super readers.

Or when your three younger brothers are gaining on you.

Mrs. Stickler handed me a note that explained the Green Group. My parents would have to sign this note.[1]

It didn't end there. That day, my nose had been tickling. I rubbed it. It still tickled. I scratched it. It still tickled. It started to feel like there was something dangling on the end of it. I felt the end of my nose for stray nose crust. Nothing. But just then, Mrs. Stickler looked my way.

"Curious, come here," she said.

I walked to her desk.

"Yes?" I said.

"Curious," she said, "you are in the fourth grade now. It is time for you to act more *appropriate*. Don't pick your nose, and go wash your hands."

I wasn't picking my nose! And what was she talking about being *appropriate*?

----

1   This is a footnote. Scientists like footnotes. Footnotes add a little more information. So here is that information: Even though I am not a super-human reader, I am pretty smart. I just like to take my time at reading. That should not be grounds for reading group demotion. Demotion is a fancy word for FLUNK!

And why are teachers so scared of germs? Should I be afraid of germs?

Mrs. Stickler is about 103 years old. Her ideas might be older. But I kept my mouth shut. I am good at that.

I walked to the sink in the back of the room. At least she hadn't said anything in front of everybody.

But the final blow came when Mrs. Stickler handed out blank sheets of white paper. She told us to take out our colored pencils.

"Who likes to draw? Let's draw a picture of what you want to be when you grow up," she said.

This was the fourth grade! We weren't kindergartners. Why were we coloring pictures? Besides, growing up was not going to happen for a long time.

The more I thought about growing up, the more upset I got. I had never really thought about what I wanted to be. Now I would have to decide.

I could teach English like my mother. But she loves English, and I don't even like books.

I didn't want to teach English.

I could be a chef — but can you imagine how many dishes I'd have to wash?

I'd love to join the Olympic track team. But let's face it — I am not very quick or coordinated.

Everyone was scribbling away. I sat and stared ahead. I looked at Mrs. Stickler's perfectly curled hair and *appropriate* outfit. I definitely didn't want to teach fourth grade.

I could be a doctor or a nurse like Aunt Dolly. But I like blood even less than books.

"Five more minutes!" said Mrs. Stickler. She was rummaging around in the top drawer of her desk.

I was running out of career choices — and time. Finally, I decided I would have to be a teacher. Not because my mother is a teacher, but because teaching doesn't involve blood. And I could focus on Mrs. Stickler's desk — the straight lines might be easy to draw.

I drew a very good picture of a desk. I worked hard on getting that desk just right. It had tight corners and precise dovetail joints.[2]

---

2   Dovetail joints have interlocking notches. These help hold pieces of wood together. They have a trapezoidal shape – kind of like a dove's tail. So now you know why they are called that.

Then I drew several teacher items on the desk. I drew an apple, a book, and an industrial-sized bottle of hand sanitizer. Teachers can handle kids, but they are terrified of germs.

"Four more minutes!" said Mrs. Stickler. I studied her. As she opened another drawer, I saw a pair of rubber gloves. I wondered when she would use those.

I sketched my future self sitting behind the desk. My future self had a very neat and short hairstyle — not long and tangly like it is now.[3]

My future self was still tall, but not so geeky and skinny. I drew a bluish green necklace to match my eyes. I even drew a nice plain blue dress. No more hand-me-downs. I was looking very *appropriate*, I might add.

But I could not bring myself to put a smile on my future face. My life would be spent scraping gum and

---

3   The McCarthys don't pay for haircuts. With seven kids, my parents have to economize. So our options are letting our hair grow long, letting Dad cut it in the shape of a bowl, or letting Dad give it a buzz cut. I'll bet you can guess my choice.

wiping boogers off desks. Maybe that's why Mrs. Stickler had rubber gloves.

The only good thing about being a teacher would be recess. But recess would not be fun either. I might have to yell at the kids on the playground. And make them go wash their hands after picking boogers.

Mrs. Stickler collected the pictures. Then she pumped her hand sanitizer three times and smeared it around her hands.

Then she handed out another blank sheet of paper. This exercise was not finished.

She said, "Because this is Fiction Week, I want you to use your imagination. Fiction is all about imagination. This time, if you are a girl, draw a picture of what you would be if you were a boy. If you are a boy, draw a picture of what you would be if you were a girl."

What?!

A girl can do any job a boy can do! Mrs. Stickler must be from the 1920s.[4]

I never expected to make a career choice in fourth grade. But if this was Fiction Week, maybe I *could* be an Olympic runner. Maybe I didn't have to settle for being a teacher. Maybe I didn't even have to be *appropriate*! I could be anything. Even the president of the United States! I drew a picture of the White House with puffy clouds in the sky above.[5]

As I perfected the clouds, I thought about the president. Presidents shake a lot of hands. I wondered if presidents were like teachers and used a lot of hand sanitizer.

The president also has to talk to a lot of people. Maybe I wasn't cut out to be president. I am more of a quiet observer.

"Three more minutes!" said Mrs. Stickler.

---

4   Back in the 1920s, some girls had limited career choices. Mom, teacher, or nurse. But this is not historical fiction, so let's move on.
5   They were cumulus clouds. Cumulus clouds look like cotton balls. Or, if you are hungry, more like a head of cauliflower.

I quickly drew the president on the South Lawn, pinning a medal on me. It was the National Medal of Science.

I could be a scientist. Scientists solve problems. Maybe I would be able to solve some of my own. And my first problem was to figure out how to become a scientist.

2

I walked home from the bus stop, trailing behind
my sister, Anne. Two of my three younger brothers
walked behind me. I was in a good mood because
of my new future career prospects. I wanted to start
being a scientist right away.

Scientists figure stuff out. Maybe I could figure
out what kinds of germs Mrs. Stickler was killing
with her hand sanitizer. Maybe I could figure out how
to get out of the Green Group.

But I shuffled slower when I remembered the note
from Mrs. Stickler. Soon my parents would read all
about the Green Group.

I decided to practice my science skills. I practiced observing. Observing seemed like a good way to distract myself from my Green Group problem.

Walking up to the house, I observed that our house was the biggest on the block. Not the nicest, just the biggest. Dad thought of our house as an engineering experiment. With each new kid, he added something.

The latest addition was when Edison, my youngest brother, was born. Dad decided it was time for a second bathroom. This one would have four sinks. This last experiment isn't finished, though. Right now it's just a great storage area.

Our house also stands out because of the color. It is bright blue with purple shutters in a row of beige houses. The purple shutters were Mom's idea.

Walking into the house, I observed the red carpet with wild paisley designs. The carpet is the type you see in hotels.

Dad said the wild patterns were designed to hide spills and dirt. That's an important design element in this family. Our flowered sofa is proof that my parents are not interior decorators.

I observed Dad. He was in the kitchen. Edison was following him around. They were lining up some interesting vegetables on the counter.

Dad is an engineer, but he retired early. That means he has a lot of time to hang out with us kids. Also, it means that Mom can work full time as an English professor. Well, she probably could have done that years ago, but it's kind of expensive to put seven kids in daycare.

It is a bit unusual having a dad who is retired, but it is also a lot of fun. Especially hanging around the kitchen with him.

"You have to think in terms of function," Dad was saying.

Dad organizes his kitchen like Command Central.[6] He lines up bowls by size. He stores eating utensils in one drawer. He puts cooking utensils in another.

"Why?" asked Edison.

"Because it is efficient," said Dad.

"Why?" asked Edison.

---

6   Command Central is usually a military facility. It is a room where plans are made for a war. In this case, it is used to control the activities for a family with seven unruly kids.

Dad grabbed his clipboard. He started sketching a diagram for Edison.

Feeling like this was the perfect chance, I handed Dad my note and turned to leave.

"Halt!" said Dad.[7]

"Yes?" I said, turning slowly.

"What is this?" he asked.

Thinking quickly, I said, "Mrs. Stickler is putting me in the Green Reading Group because I need to focus more on science."

"Why?" said Dad.

"Because I have to think in terms of function," I said.

"Why?" said Dad.

"Because that is the only way I will get the National Medal of Science," I said.

Luckily for me, having six brothers and sisters means it is never long before a fight breaks out.

---

7   A German military command that means "Stop!" My dad is Irish. Not German.

We heard the front door slam. That meant my two oldest sisters, Charlotte and Emily, were home.

"Put your backpack away, John Glenn!" bossed Charlotte. I heard muffled screams. A muddy boot flew through the kitchen.

Dad quickly signed the note. Then he left Command Central to enter battle.

I turned and walked past the orange counters.

Past the art wall — where Mom hung all our school projects.

Past the coat hooks — two for each of the McCarthys.

Then I slipped up the back stairs to my quarters.[8]

---

8   Quarters are what military people call the place where they sleep. I couldn't say "my room." In a family this size, no one has their own room.

3

Monday, 6:00 p.m.

That night at dinner, I had another chance to practice being a scientist. I decided to observe my family.

My parents made an agreement before they had kids. Mom would name the girls. Dad would name the boys.

Mom started naming the girls after famous authors. So, Charlotte, Emily, and Anne were named after three sisters who were famous authors. They match up exactly with the birth order of the Brontë sisters. The Brontë sisters wrote some books that the Green Group will never read.

By the time I came around, it was getting obvious that they might be stuck with more girls than boys.

So Dad got to pick my name. He named me Curie

after Marie Curie. But everyone calls me Curious.[9]

Back to my observations. I started with observing

Charlotte. Charlotte is thirteen. She thinks she's

pretty important because she's the oldest.

----

9   Marie Curie was a famous scientist, but I didn't find that out until later. I just
figured that the Brontës were out of sisters.

She has long, dark hair that is always shiny. It is always perfectly combed. Even her teeth are perfectly straight. Or they will be now that she has braces.

Charlotte was folding the napkins in perfect rectangles. Charlotte is known for her proper napkin folding, fork placement, and polite words.

She has perfect table manners. She is *appropriate*. Mrs. Stickler would love her.

I observed Emily. Emily is twelve. She has reddish hair. It's not as straight as Charlotte's, but she keeps it perfectly neat too. Emily can be a bit eccentric in her clothing choices.[10]

Emily was putting plates on the table. She counted the plates in Spanish. She put a napkin on her head. She's a bit weird.

I observed Anne. Anne is eleven. She has long hair that she keeps in a neat ponytail. But she also has bangs. She cuts them herself. This time she got them straight, but sometimes she doesn't.

Anne put the forks on the left side of the plates. Then she looked at Emily and asked, "What did the mayo say to the ketchup?"

We all waited.

"Don't look! I am dressing!" Anne laughed.

---

10   According to my dictionary, eccentric means strange. But strange in a charming way. Most people like Emily. Even if she is charmingly strange.

"Mayo can't talk," said Ben, who is five.

Dad says a good engineer sets goals. Maybe scientists do that too. My goal tonight was to go unnoticed. I didn't want any questions about the Green Group.

Going unnoticed is easy in a large family. Especially when you are the middle child. Having three younger brothers also comes in handy.

My younger brothers have no table manners.

John Glenn is eight. He is blond-haired and blue-eyed. My parents think he is an angel. Except when he burps.[11]

Ben comes next. Ben always looks serious. He wears glasses like Dad. His hair is cut very short like Dad's too. Ben doesn't like it when his hair gets longer than two centimeters.

Exactly two centimeters.

----

11   John Glenn is named after the first *American* astronaut to orbit the Earth. He shouldn't complain. At least his name sounds better than Yuri Gagarin, the first human to orbit the Earth. But I think naming him Albert after the first primate in space might have been more *appropriate*.

Ben wears the same shirt every day — blue with a white stripe. Well, not really. Mom bought two shirts that are the same, so he can have clean clothes.

Ben separates his food into groups. He doesn't like his food to touch and sometimes shoves it off the end of his plate.

Then there is Edison. Edison is four. He doesn't go to school yet. He doesn't care about haircuts or clothes or manners. Edison spills more food on the floor than he puts in his mouth. I used to try to convince my parents that we should get a dog. A dog could clean up after the boys. It could just hang out under the table. But Mom said that at least kids grow up. Dogs never do. She has a point.

I observed our kitchen habitat.[12] We have an old oak library table. Mom got it at a library sale. She goes to the library sale on the last day, because she can get a bag of used books for four dollars.

---

12 A habitat is a word that scientists use for the home of animals or plants. Or in this case, my family.

She gets lots of classic books for my sisters, like *Little House on the Prairie* and *Treasure Island*. She gets lots of picture books for my brothers, like *Green Eggs and Ham* and *The Snotty Book of Snot*.[13]

And one time, when Mom was at the library sale, she talked them out of a table. Maybe she got it for four dollars.

The table is huge. The whole family can sit around it at the same time. But the really cool thing about this table is that it has drawers along each side. They are great places to hide some of the questionable ingredients that come with dinner. My theory is that the drawers were meant to hold pencils and papers, not black olives and brussels sprouts.

That night, as Dad began to put dinner on the table, I decided to make my first hypothesis.[14]

----

13   These are real books – I am not kidding. I might have to read them someday. They both sound like they would be good references for a scientist who wants to study slimy green stuff.
14   A hypothesis is basically a guess that is based on limited evidence. My job as a scientist is to gather more evidence.

My hypothesis was this: John Glenn would get Mom and Dad's attention before Charlotte. He is an excellent burper, after all.

In order to support this hypothesis, I continued to observe. Charlotte unfolded her napkin. She placed it neatly in her lap. She rested her wrists, not her elbows, on the table.

Dad made black bean salad for Meatless Monday.[15]

Black beans are fine, except John Glenn does not like them. I switched my observations to John Glenn.

I looked at his eyes first. They were wide. They were darting around the room. I looked at his mouth. It was all frowny, like he was about to throw up.

Mom rushed in from work. She said, "Let the wild rumpus start!"

Dad looked at the clock. Everything in our house is timed and precise, like a well-oiled machine.

---

15   Scientists think going meatless once a week can reduce the risk of disease. Plus it's good for the environment. The McCarthys are not concerned with disease. They are concerned with the cost of meat. But when you get to the end of this book, you might think they should be more concerned about disease.

John Glenn was watching Dad. As soon as Dad looked at the clock, John Glenn slipped his black beans into the drawer beneath his spot at the table. When Dad turned back he saw Charlotte dabbing her lips with her napkin. He smiled.

Charlotte was the one who got Dad's attention that night.

Apparently, a hypothesis is not always correct.

4

I made a mistake with my first hypothesis. Maybe I hadn't made enough observations.

I walked down to the boys' room. Mom reads to us every night. She reads in the boys' room because Edison always falls asleep before she finishes.

I wanted to improve my observation skills, so I observed Mom.

She is taller than Dad.

She has long, blond hair.

Her hair was pulled back in a neat French braid.

She was wearing a purple shirt.

That night Mom was reading *Oliver Twist*. She is a great reader. She does all the voices. My older sisters even come in to listen some nights.

Last week she read *Charlie and the Chocolate Factory*. Mom loves classics. Classics are books that are usually written by dead people.

Lately, Mom has been unusually interested in books about little boys who can't get enough to eat. I'll bet Oliver and Charlie wouldn't complain about black bean salad.[16]

While Mom was reading, I made a survey of the room. Dad had made a sort of triple bunk for the boys. It isn't three beds on top of each other — that wouldn't have fit. Dad engineered the triple bunk to fit the room perfectly. John Glenn's bunk is on top. Ben and Edison's beds are under at the same level, but they stick out in different directions. Dad probably hadn't planned on John Glenn using his bunk as a platform. He jumped down onto Ben's bed.

"John Glenn, stay on your own bed," said Mom.

---

16   *Oliver Twist* is a classic book by Charles Dickens. Oliver is an orphan who only gets mush. *Charlie and the Chocolate Factory* is a book by Roald Dahl. In this book people only eat cabbage and chocolate. Black bean salad might be a nice change of pace.

John Glenn crawled back up to the top bunk. Mom
continued to read. But John Glenn dangled his legs
over the side, swiping Ben's head with his foot.

I wondered how many kicks it would take for Ben and John Glenn to get in a fight.

I thought about making another hypothesis. But I needed to do a little more research first. If I got too many hypotheses wrong, my future as a scientist might be at risk.

5

Tuesday, 7:45 a.m.

I snatched my library book out of Edison's hands.
I checked my nose to make sure there was nothing
dangling from it. I checked my pockets for extra
tissues. Then I followed Anne, John Glenn, and Ben
out the front door.

It was Library Day. Mrs. Stickler made this an all-
day affair. She really likes books. I don't know who is
more obsessed with books: Mrs. Stickler or Mom.

Mrs. Stickler started the day by talking about
fiction genres.[17]

After that, she explained her book rules. The first
book rule was:

Draw pictures on paper, not in books!

----

17   It was Fiction Week, remember? If you are in fourth, fifth, or sixth grade, you
know all about genres. If you are in second or third grade, a genre is a type of book. Like
mysteries, science fiction, or romance. You are not likely to find much romance in an
elementary school.

Mrs. Stickler probably used to teach kindergarten. Most fourth graders already know about book rules. Mrs. Stickler read a chapter out of *Horrible Harry and the Green Slime*. I know all about Harry. My first-grade teacher read that book to us.[18]

Since I was familiar with the story, my mind wandered. I wished we could make the green slime. But Mrs. Stickler wouldn't let us do that in class. She would be worried about germs. She would probably use those rubber gloves . . .

After she finished reading, Mrs. Stickler led us to the library.

We returned last week's books and headed to the fiction section. Mrs. Stickler reminded us about Fiction Week.

"You may each pick out two fiction books. They must be two different genres," she said. But as soon as Mrs. Stickler looked away, I crept to the back shelves.

---

18 *Horrible Harry and the Green Slime* is a book by Suzy Kline. If you are a fourth grader, you probably already know that.

I bent my knees a bit, so she would not see the top of my head moving behind the shelving. I crept along the back wall to the nonfiction section. I was pretty sure that scientists read nonfiction.

I stayed low as I searched for the 500s.[19]

---
19   The numbers on nonfiction books are part of the Dewey decimal system. The 500s are where you find science and math books. The system was named after Melvil Dewey, an American librarian. He developed this system in 1876. I wonder if Mrs. Stickler knew him.

I passed up books called *Electricity* and *How Batteries Work.* I found several books on geology. Those looked interesting. And the books on bats and insects looked like they might be good. There was a book on apes and other primates. Maybe it would come in handy. I could use it to do some research on my younger brothers.

I looked at a book on snails. Then I found a book called *Living in a Bacterial World.* I finally settled on *Bacteria and Fungi: Your Guide to Germs.* That book might also come in handy for little-brother research. Maybe there was some bacteria growing in the drawers beneath our kitchen table. I thought the book might also help me figure out why teachers were so scared of germs.[20]

I crawled back to the fiction section and found a book called *Snot Soup.* That might help me figure out if there was a connection between germs and snot.

---

20   Bacteria are tiny living things that are everywhere. You could also call them germs, or maybe cooties.

Scientists are good at making connections. Maybe making connections is how you become a scientist.

I tried to look calm. I made sure my nose was clean and that there was nothing crusty dangling from it. I didn't want to stand out, or someone might notice I was checking out nonfiction books during Fiction Week. Then I lined up to check out.

When it was my turn, I put my books on the counter. Mr. Grumpus, the librarian, smiled when he saw my books. I guess he approved of my choices.

6

Tuesday, 5:31 p.m.

It was Taco Tuesday. Dad showed the boys and me how to line up all the ingredients in the right order. Dad made his tacos like an engineer. He mixed the tomato chunks into the meat.

"Why?" asked Edison.

"Because it's efficient," said Dad. "It saves time. And there are fewer dishes to wash."

Emily walked through the kitchen. She had her head in a book as she walked toward the table. She looked up and said, "Yum. Tacos. *MUCHOS* tacos."[21]

Mom walked in, dumped her pile of books on the counter, and gave Dad a big smooch.[22]

---

21 After only a few days of her new middle school Spanish class, Emily doesn't really speak Spanish. She just likes to pretend she does. Emily is weird.

22 Apparently, Mom might love Dad as much as her books. But do you ever wonder how many germs are swapped with the average kiss? According to *Guide to Germs*, it is approximately 80 million.

We settled around the table for dinner. Or at least the girls were settled — the boys were still shoving each other off their chairs.

"How was school?" Mom asked.

"Exactly as I expected," said Charlotte.

"*FABULOSO!*" shouted Emily.

"What food do math teachers eat?" asked Anne.

I stayed quiet, in order to observe.

"I'm hungry!" shouted John Glenn.

"Math teachers eat breakfast, lunch, and dinner," said Ben.[23]

"OUCH!" shouted Edison as he slipped and fell out of his chair.

"Settle down," said Dad as he brought dinner to the table.

I wondered if I should make a new hypothesis. I could make a hypothesis about bacteria. Bacteria sounded scientific.

----
23   Anne tells a lot of jokes and I have heard this one before. Math teachers eat square meals. Get it?

I wondered how much bacteria might grow in John Glenn's drawer by the end of the week. But I wasn't sure how to measure bacteria. And lots of bacteria are too small to see. I wondered if I could be a scientist without a microscope.

I decided to stick with my original hypothesis: John Glenn would get Mom and Dad's attention.

Maybe he wouldn't get their attention first, but he was bound to get their attention by the end of the week. That seemed like an easier thing to prove than trying to see microscopic bacteria.

I kept John Glenn under observation. Dad's tomato efficiency was a problem for John Glenn. He can't stand tomatoes.

He looked down at his plate and then asked for ketchup. He smothered his taco in ketchup. It was an attempt to hide all the tomato chunks. This was not logical, because ketchup is made out of tomatoes.[24]

I looked at Ben, who had opened his taco. He put the tomato chunks in a separate pile.

I looked at Edison, who was dropping pieces of taco shell on the floor. Maybe he was feeding the dog.[25]

I returned to my observation of John Glenn. Even with the ketchup on top, I noticed he was getting squirmy about the chunky tomato tacos.

Emily was sneaking peeks at the book in her lap.

Anne was doing the same.

Charlotte was eating her tacos with a fork. She needed to eat little bits. She didn't want pieces of food stuck in her braces.

----

24 Approximately 72 tomatoes per bottle.
25 But we don't have a dog. Remember?

Dad looked at Charlotte and smiled. At that moment, I saw John Glenn out of the corner of my eye. He looked at Dad. Then he quickly scraped the meat out of his taco. I heard it plop into the drawer. Right on top of the black beans.

Apparently Mom and Dad didn't hear the plop. They didn't even look John Glenn's way. I wondered how long successful scientists stuck with the same hypothesis.

7

Wednesday, 1:42 p.m.

In *Guide to Germs*, it says that scientists should brainstorm. That's kind of like daydreaming. For a scientist, daydreaming is as powerful as observation. I decided I would practice daydreaming.

We were in our reading groups. The Green Group was reading *Sally's Trip to the Store*. Sally's trip wasn't very exciting, so it was the perfect opportunity for me to practice daydreaming. I daydreamed about Sally taking a more exciting trip to Mars.

The Red Group returned from an exciting trip to the lavatory. Mrs. Stickler has her students take group bathroom breaks. It's like the buddy system. Probably to make sure they wash their hands. If someone forgets to wash, someone else will tattle. I daydreamed about all the millions of bacteria on their hands. I daydreamed about being a scientist who studies bacteria.

"I hope everyone washed their hands with *lots* of soap," said Mrs. Stickler. Remember, teachers are scared of germs. I daydreamed about giant germs invading the school. "Finish up your reading," said Mrs. Stickler. "Then take out your art supplies."

The Green Group finished *Sally's Trip to the Store*. Then we searched for our art supplies.

I looked in my desk. I saw a sad pile of markers. When you are in a family with seven kids, you get lots of hand-me-downs. And I don't just mean clothes. I mean school supplies.

I had three blue markers, one red marker, one brown marker, and one yellow marker. And the yellow marker was dried out. I took the cap off one of the blue markers to check for dryness. I daydreamed about being an only child. An only child with a brand-new box of markers.

"You'll need your markers and your drawing pads," said Mrs. Stickler.

"NOW!" she said, this time right behind me. The blue marker I was holding streaked across page 23 of *Sally's Trip to the Store*. Right across Sally's face.

"Curious McCarthy!" she snapped. "We draw pictures on paper, not in books!"

Now I was in big trouble. Apparently, I am no good at daydreaming either. Maybe I am just not cut out to be a scientist. Maybe I should be a criminal.[26]

Mrs. Stickler took my arm and marched me down to the principal's office.

She whisked me past the secretary. Past the orange chairs filled with naughty kids. Past John Glenn, who was waiting in one of those chairs.

That was an interesting observation. Maybe daydreaming wasn't working for me today. But I could always go back to observing.

---

26 This blue-marker disaster might be a felony. A felony is a serious crime that will get you sent to prison. Or an all-expenses-paid trip to the principal's office.

Principal Cornforth sent me home with a note. Another note for my parents to sign.

"Now, Curious," he said, looking down at me. "I know you want to be a scientist when you grow up. But scientists have to spend their time in class and not in the principal's office."

I hadn't said anything to Mr. Cornforth about being a scientist. How did he know?

On my way home that day, I daydreamed about the teachers' lounge. I pictured Mrs. Stickler and Mr. Cornforth talking about all the ways they would make life miserable for the kids at Hilltop. I imagined them laughing over my National Medal of Science picture. They probably passed it around to all the other teachers. Maybe there was a big plan to change my mind. Maybe they were trying to make me become a teacher instead.

But I had a plan. I was going to work hard to become a scientist. Starting right away.

That night, I would wait until after John Glenn handed Dad his note from the principal.

I didn't know what John Glenn did to get himself sent to the principal's office. But I was sure it involved something worse than a blue marker. Then maybe my note would not seem so bad.

But best of all, I'd finally have some support for my hypothesis. John Glenn's bad behavior would get my parents' attention. And I would be a successful scientist.

8

Wednesday, 4:02 p.m.

"We are having an SSS meeting. Now," Anne whispered in my ear.

The SSS stands for the Secret Sister Society. The McCarthy sisters held this meeting a few times a month. The meetings were top secret. No parents allowed. No brothers allowed.

I walked quietly to the back stairs and up to our quarters. Anne tiptoed behind me. Emily and Charlotte were already in our room.

I don't really fit in with the SSS. My perfect sisters sometimes talk about kicking me out. That would be fine with me. I need more time to be a scientist anyway.

But sometimes I am useful. I keep notes in the secret notebook.

That day, I would pretend it was my scientific journal. I would record the events just like a *real* scientist would.

"Call to order," said Charlotte. "Emily, you take notes. The notes that Curious took last time were too messy." Charlotte handed Emily the secret notebook.

Apparently, I was not as useful as I thought.[27]

"*No problemo!*" said Emily.

"We have to talk about our brothers," said Charlotte. "They are a threat to family harmony."

I watched over Emily's shoulder as she wrote in the secret notebook. She did not doodle.

We started the SSS when Mom went back to work. Charlotte said that our home life would fall to pieces without Mom around to keep the boys in line. The purpose of the SSS was to maintain family harmony.

"I've noticed that John Glenn is shoving his dinner into a drawer under the table," said Charlotte.

----

27   For the record, my notes are NOT messy. I just like to doodle a little bit. Scientists believe that doodling helps you focus and improves your memory.

"Mom and Dad are going to find a week's worth of disgusting food in John Glenn's drawer. Ben and Edison are bound to copy him. Then we'll all be in trouble. Mom might think that Dad's not doing a good job. Dad might get fed up and go back to work. Edison would be sent to daycare. The rest of you would be signed up for after-school programs. Like the homework lab. Or broomball."[28]

Charlotte looked straight at me. "Someone has to tattle on John Glenn," she finished.

So that was it. The SSS wanted me to be the one to tell on John Glenn. My stomach felt queasy.

"But . . . ," I started to protest. Scientists aren't supposed to get involved in their experiments. How could I continue to be a silent observer if I took an action that would affect my hypothesis?

Charlotte said, "Meeting adjourned." She grabbed the secret notebook and turned to walk away.

---

28   Broomball is a sport where you sweep a ball over the ice. And if I were taking the notes, I would document this as a chain reaction. Scientists use the term chain reaction to describe a series of events, where each event causes the next.

I had a problem, but Charlotte had one too. I smiled as I thought of Charlotte trying to read the minutes — Emily had written them in Spanish.

The following is what Emily wrote. Do not bother trying to understand this unless you are in seventh-grade Spanish class.

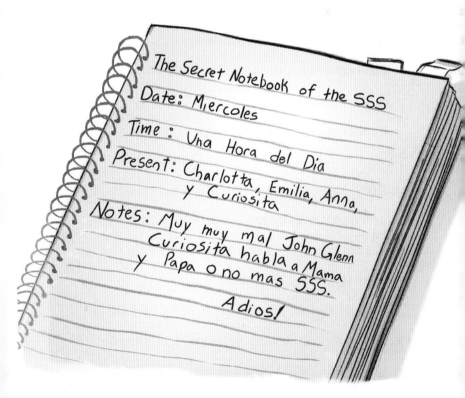

The Secret Notebook of the SSS
Date: Miercoles
Time: Una Hora del Dia
Present: Charlotta, Emilia, Anna, y Curiosita
Notes: Muy muy mal John Glenn Curiosita habla a Mama y Papa o no mas SSS.

Adios!

9

Wednesday, 4:46 p.m.

Anne and I walked downstairs. There was a delicious smell coming from the oven. Ribs. Ribs with mashed potatoes and roasted carrots — one of Dad's specialties. It is an all-around favorite.

Edison was at the table coloring. Dad was missing.

We found him out in his garden with John Glenn and Ben. The garden is surrounded by a short white fence. The fence is meant to keep the rabbits out.

"Come join me!" Dad called. Apparently, the fence isn't meant to keep kids out.

"Anne, you can pull a few carrots," said Dad. He turned to John Glenn, Ben, and me. "I need nine potatoes. You can each pull three."

We climbed over the fence. This was our chance to play in the dirt. According to *Guide to Germs*, one spoonful of dirt might have one billion bacteria.[29]

We picked the potatoes. Then John Glenn, Ben, and I brought them to the kitchen sink. Anne and Dad were still pulling carrots.

"Edison," said John Glenn. "Come and help us build a Lego tower." And Edison followed John Glenn and Ben out of the room.

I should have reminded them to wash, but this was my chance. I let them walk away with their microbe-covered hands so I could check out the bacteria in John Glenn's drawer. I needed to work harder if I wanted to be a scientist.

I checked to make sure no one was watching and walked over to the table. I looked carefully at John Glenn's drawer. I couldn't see anything spilling out of it.

----
29   That means a cup of soil from this garden would have more bacteria than there are humans on Earth. Soil is a crowded place.

I looked underneath. I saw a wad of gum. I wondered if John Glenn put it there or if it was there when Mom bought the table. Gross. That might have been really old gum. It might have been an antique.[30]

I quietly slid the drawer open.

The smell of the black beans hit me right away. I wasn't sure if that meant bacteria were taking over or if it was just the spices Dad used.

I remembered Mrs. Stickler's rubber gloves. So before I went any further, I got some gloves from under the kitchen sink. With the gloves, I felt more like a scientist. As I slid the drawer open further, I saw a math worksheet from last year. I saw a pencil with teeth marks on it.

On top of the math worksheet, I saw the ketchup-covered taco meat from yesterday. I picked up the pencil and poked at it. The pencil slid into it easily. It was crusty on the outside but soft on the inside. Yuck.

----

30   An antique is something that is really old. Like gum on the underside of a table. I wonder if Mrs. Stickler is an antique. Maybe it's her gum from about 1922.

I turned toward the other side of the drawer and spotted a hot dog. It sat inside its bun and looked as good as new. I didn't even *remember* having hot dogs. Only Mom makes hot dogs, and she hadn't cooked in a long time.

I took the pencil and poked at the hot dog. It was hard. I poked at the bun. It was hard too. I wondered if it was petrified.[31]

31 Petrified means that it changed into stone. Like some dinosaur bones after about 65 million years . . . or a hot dog after 65 days.

I thought about cleaning up the bacteria-filled drawer. Maybe it would get Charlotte off my back. But this experiment was kind of cool. I was curious. I wondered how long it would take for the taco meat to petrify. Maybe this could be a new hypothesis?

I heard Dad and Anne coming in from the backyard. I quickly shut the drawer. I shoved the gloves under the table and practiced looking innocent.

10

Wednesday, 5:48 p.m.

A little while later, Dad was back in Command Central cutting potatoes and carrots. I hung around, waiting for the right moment.

"*Uno, dos, tres* . . . " Emily counted out nine napkins in Spanish. Then she folded the napkins into squares. Well, not squares exactly. The sides were not equal.[32]

Anne was showing Ben where to put the forks and knives. "The fork goes on the left," said Anne. "Left and fork both have four letters."

"That is not a good reason," said Ben.

Anne rolled her eyes and continued, "The knife and spoon go on the right. Knife, spoon, and right all have five letters."

---

32 Emily is not as good as Charlotte with a napkin. And Emily is weird.

Anne is going to make a great teacher — if she can stop rolling her eyes.

"But how many letters does napkin have?" asked Ben.

Before Anne could answer, Dad shouted, "Dinner's ready!"

We all rushed around the table to our spots. Dad passed around the plates. Each plate had one serving of mashed potatoes, two ribs, and three roasted carrots.[33]

We waited for Mom to get home before we started eating. Our mouths were watering. Except for John Glenn's. He would not eat a roasted carrot even if you paid him ten dollars. He stared down at his plate.

I knew where John Glenn wanted to put those three roasted carrots. They would go nicely with the black bean salad and taco meat.

---

33   This is called rationing. That's when everyone gets a fixed amount of something. Rationing is important so that you don't run out of stuff too soon. Rationing is important during wars. Because a country might run out of bread or steel before the war is over. Rationing is also important in large families. Because you might run out of food before dinner is over . . . except for the roasted carrots . . . we usually don't run out of those.

He must have needed a distraction, because he blurted out, "Curious was sent to the principal's office today!"

So much for going unnoticed. And so much for tattling on John Glenn first. As Dad looked my way, John Glenn slipped the carrots into the drawer on top of the tacos and black beans.

"I see," said Dad.

I froze and couldn't think of anything to say. And then my mind wandered. I daydreamed about the carrots hitting the mound of taco meat. I wondered if it would affect the petrification rate.

"What is this about, Curious?" asked Dad.

I knew he wasn't asking about the carrot torpedoes, but I couldn't help thinking about them. Scientists are curious.

Luckily, Mom walked in and plopped down her huge pile of books. This set a chain reaction into motion.

The books shook the table, causing the ketchup bottle to tip over. The ketchup shot out of the top of the bottle, hitting Dad in the face.[34]

Mom and Dad looked at each other. Everyone was silent. We waited to see what would happen.

John Glenn let out a huge burp. *That should get Mom and Dad's attention . . .*

----

34   Another chain reaction. And ketchup is served at every McCarthy meal, in case you are wondering.

Charlotte politely said, "May I have more carrots please?"

Dad turned his ketchup-covered face toward her and smiled.

And Mom let out a laugh and smiled too.

11

Thursday, 7:26 a.m.

I walked down the stairs and was greeted with Dad's favorite breakfast — fried-egg sandwiches. Dad ate his with a fork.

"Why?" asked Edison.

"Because I can slice off a precise amount of toast and egg. An exact square. A square has equal sides," Dad said.

I watched as he did this. He followed each precise forkful with a slurp of black coffee. I wondered why he didn't measure the coffee with a measuring spoon.

Maybe I should tell on John Glenn now, I thought. *Open the drawer, show Dad, and get it over with.*

Or maybe not. Dad might remember to ask about my trip to the principal's office.

I was especially worried about that. So I decided to eat as quietly as possible.

My stomach was in knots. The runny eggs didn't help. But I realized Dad's mind was somewhere else. He was enjoying his precise breakfast.

12

Thursday, 8:15 a.m.

In class, Mrs. Stickler was a little jumpy when she heard me sneeze. I quickly sniffled so my nose didn't drip.

"Please use the tissues for your nose issues!" she announced to the class.[35]

I was reaching into my desk when a tissue appeared in front of my face. The tissue was connected to a hand. The hand was connected to the girl sitting in the desk next to me.

I looked at Lin Tran like I hadn't seen her before — and I hadn't. I had failed to observe the girl sitting in the desk next to me for the last two weeks.

Apparently I was not very good at observing.

---

35   Have I mentioned how much they like rules at Hilltop?

Maybe I am not a very good scientist. I guess being a good scientist takes a lot of practice.

I took the tissue from Lin. She smiled. Then Mrs. Stickler had us get up and scoot our desks a little farther apart. Sharing tissues might be okay. But she didn't want us sharing germs.

13

Thursday, 12:15 p.m.

I sat in the cafeteria with the rest of the cold-lunch crowd. This crowd included Lin Tran. She smiled. I sat down across from her.

Robin Finch, the girl on my left, scooted away from me a bit. I formed a theory that Lin might make a better friend than Robin.

I opened my brown bag.[36]

I had an egg-salad sandwich. The smell of the egg salad made me a little sick. Egg overload.

It's too bad cafeteria tables don't have drawers. I felt along underneath the table just in case. I felt a small lump of something crusted to the bottom of the table. Gross. Probably gum.

Or boogers.

36　A reused brown bag, I observed.

Mrs. Stickler's hand sanitizer might not be such a bad idea.

I observed Lin as she took out a spoon that wasn't even plastic. Her parents must really trust her.

I observed Robin as she took out a matching set of plastic containers. She opened each container and stacked the lids neatly. She had a healthy assortment of nuts and vegetables.

After lunch, Mrs. Stickler announced that we were going to continue Fiction Week by putting on a play.

"Most plays are fiction. They are a good way to use your imagination," she said.

We would start practicing our parts tomorrow. Then in a few weeks, we would perform for our parents. But the first order of business was to paint the background. Mrs. Stickler pointed to some huge sheets of cardboard at the back of the classroom.

She assigned spots along the cardboard. This would be the backdrop for our play. She gave us all tempera paints.[37]

Mrs. Stickler had already used a pencil to draw some shapes on the cardboard.

"Make sure to stay inside the lines," she said as she paced back and forth.

I brushed brown tempera paint into the shape of a tree. The strong odor of egg paint brought back memories of lunch. Suddenly I felt a tingly feeling in my mouth.

I thought I should run to the bathroom. But Mrs. Stickler has rules about bathroom breaks. Before I had time to ask permission, I threw up all over the floor.

Mrs. Stickler shot into action right away. She called all the kids to line up against the far wall by the windows.

----

37   Tempera is also known as egg tempera. It is a paint consisting of colored pigments usually mixed with a glutinous (or slimy) material such as egg yolk. The school version of tempera paint is not really made with eggs anymore. But it still stinks.

She grabbed my arm and guided me down to the nurse's office.[38]

Through the haze of sickness, I thought I saw John Glenn sitting on the orange plastic chairs outside Principal Cornforth's office again. But the next thing I knew, Dad was leading me out to the car. Edison followed behind.

"We've got to remember to wash our hands," Dad said as he opened the back door.

"Why?" asked Edison.

"To wash away any bacteria," Dad said.

"Why?" asked Edison.

But I didn't hear Dad's answer. I was too busy daydreaming about bacteria. I wondered which bacteria made me barf.

----

38 With her rubber-gloved hands, in case you were wondering. She was not about to let any germs infect her classroom.

14

Thursday, 2:45 p.m.

"Your father tells me you want to be a scientist,"
Aunt Dolly said. She liked to stop by in the afternoons
for coffee.

Aunt Dolly brought popsicles. Some people think
popsicles make you feel better when you are sick. But
Aunt Dolly brought them all the time.

I was in the kitchen, enjoying my popsicle. And
the fact that I got out of a few hours of school. I felt
much better, but I wasn't about to let Dad know that.

"What kind of scientist?" asked Aunt Dolly.

"Maybe a biologist," I said. "It would be fun to
study living things. Like people and bacteria."

"Oh, I work with a radiologist," she said. "What a
coincidence."[39]

----

39   This is not what I would call a coincidence. A biologist studies life. A radiologist is
a kind of doctor. A word ending in -*ology* or -*ologist* just means "an area of study." I am
not going to be a doctor. I don't like blood, remember?

I observed Aunt Dolly as she sipped her coffee. Her slurp was different than Dad's. She blew on the coffee first. Her mug said:

DON'T MESS WITH ME. I GET PAID TO STAB PEOPLE WITH SHARP OBJECTS!

"Maybe you'd like to be a dendrologist," said Dad. "You like trees."[40]

---

40 Dendrology is the study of trees. But after the tempera-paint incident, I changed my mind about trees.

"You could be a teacher," said Aunt Dolly.

"Why?" asked Edison.

"Teachers get the summer off," said Aunt Dolly. I wondered if she knew Mrs. Stickler and Mr. Cornforth. They all seemed to be trying to convince me to be a teacher.

"You can be anything you want, Curious," said Dad.

"I don't like books," I said.

"Well, it's not just teachers who read a lot of books. You'll have to read books to be a biologist," Dad said.

"Why?" asked Edison as he sat coloring a pink train.

"She will have to read books to learn all about life-forms," said Dad.

"I am going to take a nap," I said and slipped away from the table. I went upstairs so I could dream about being a scientist.

15

Thursday, 5:30 p.m.

That night, I wanted to perform an experiment. I hadn't been very successful observing or making hypotheses, so I thought I'd try something different. Scientists should probably try new things.

Mom said I had to come to the table, but I had seen spinach on the counter. So I messed my hair a little more than usual and frowned. I was trying to look sick to get out of eating dinner. It worked. Mom told me to sit on a kitchen stool and have another popsicle.

I watched as the chicken and creamed spinach was dished up. You don't have to be a scientist to guess which one John Glenn put into his drawer.

Charlotte looked at me. I supposed she was waiting for me to tattle. I ignored her. She turned to Dad and politely asked for seconds.

16

Last night's experiment was a success. So I thought I'd try it again. I left my hair uncombed and tried to look sick. But Mom made me go to school — with messy hair. I guess the same experiment does not always have the same outcome.

I had just sat down at my desk when Mrs. Stickler got a phone call. She set down the phone. "Curious," she said, "go see Mr. Grumpus in the library."

My heart beat fast. I was caught. Checking out nonfiction during Hilltop's Fiction Week must be a crime at this school. I was a book thief. But I wondered why it took all week for Mr. Grumpus to notice.

My second week in this new school was not going very well.

It didn't seem fair.

I kept getting in trouble.

I trudged out the door and down the hall.

But Mr. Grumpus knew I checked out the *Guide to Germs*. He even smiled. So why did he send for me?

I thought of all the possibilities. Maybe Mr. Grumpus was the only one who didn't laugh when he saw my National Medal of Science picture in the teacher's lounge.

Maybe *he* saw my scientific potential.

Maybe he had more germ books! I was kind of excited about that, so I walked faster.

Mr. Grumpus was at his desk. I walked up to him. I looked around for other germ books. He must have had them in a special place for me. I waited. He looked up.

Mr. Grumpus opened his top drawer.

I studied the dovetail joints on his desk as I waited for my germ books.

He handed me an envelope. "Take this to your parents," he said.

"What is it?"

"A bill," he answered.

"For what?" I asked.

"Your book."

"But why?" I asked. "I returned it."

"Because it is damaged," said Mr. Grumpus.

He reached deeper into his drawer. He pulled out last week's book. He opened the book. Across nearly every page in pink crayon it said:

NO SIDE. NO SIDE. NO SIDE.

"I didn't do that!" I said. But Mr. Grumpus held up his hand.

"The book was your responsibility," he said. "You'll have to pay for it."

I took the bill and turned to go.

"Curious," said Mr. Grumpus.

"Yes?" I said.

"Here, take the book. Your parents will want to know what they are paying for. You keep it. It will be a reminder that books are your friends."

This school had some really weird ideas about books. I wondered what Mr. Grumpus meant by books being friends. I daydreamed about Mr. Grumpus being friends with the three little pigs.

But then I remembered the trouble from the last time I daydreamed.

I walked back down the hall toward my class. I looked at the pink scribbles in the book. As I tilted the book upside down, I read those scribbles again.

EDISON. EDISON. EDISON.[41]

---

41   Technically, these letters were backward, but I have no idea how to type that.

17

Friday, 3:45 p.m.

I debated the best time to hand the bill to Dad. My last note did not go over well. But John Glenn didn't know about this note so he couldn't snitch. I could decide the best time to hand it over. I probably wouldn't get into trouble, since the evidence pointed directly to the suspect. Maybe *NO SIDE, NO SIDE, NO SIDE* would get in trouble.

Walking back to Command Central, I saw Dad showing Edison how to use the kitchen scale. He was weighing some strange-looking vegetables. John Glenn and Ben sat down to watch.

"First you need to get the tare weight," Dad was saying.[42]

"Why?" asked Edison.

----

42 Tare weight is the weight of an empty container. Looking at the pile of weird vegetables on the counter, I wished that particular container would stay empty.

"Because it is important to get an exact measurement. If you want to weigh the right amount of celery root for the celery root and pumpkin stew, you need the exact weight of the celery root, not the celery root plus its dish," Dad explained.[43]

Another great dinner, I thought. I decided to wait to hand the note to Dad.

As I walked around the corner to the back stairs, I nearly bumped in to Anne.

"Another SSS meeting," she whispered. "Now."

I took a deep breath and followed her up the stairs. I dreaded meeting with Charlotte, especially since I hadn't done what she expected. I hadn't ratted out John Glenn for putting food in his drawer.

"Call to order," Charlotte said. "This time Anne gets to take notes," she said as she handed the secret notebook to Anne and glared at Emily. I tried not to smile.

----

43   Luckily for us, Dad's garden had a bumper crop of celery root. It is an excellent source of vitamin K.

"Curious, if you don't tattle on John Glenn soon, the family harmony will be in serious trouble," Charlotte said. "The food is piling up. It is starting to stink. We are all going to get in trouble. You don't want to be signed up for broomball, do you, Curious? I sure don't. You have twenty-four hours. That's one day."

Anne was behind Charlotte and rolled her eyes. As if we didn't know how many hours were in a day without Charlotte telling us.[44]

"But . . . ," I began.

"Let's take a vote," said Charlotte. "All in favor of giving Curious twenty-four hours to tattle on John Glenn, say 'Aye.'"

There was a pause. Charlotte glared at Emily.

"Aye," said Emily.

I looked at Anne. Charlotte turned to her. Anne gave me a sorry look and said, "Aye."

----

44   Some scientists think that our days on Earth are getting longer. But I don't think they're long enough to get me out of this pinch.

"That's it," said Charlotte. "Curious, you are going to tattle before tomorrow night. If you don't, you're kicked out of the SSS."

I didn't really care if I was kicked out of the SSS, and I didn't want to tattle on John Glenn. I already had to tattle on Edison for writing in my library book. I am a scientist, not a tattler.

"Wait!" I said. But Charlotte turned. She grabbed the secret notebook away from Anne.

"Meeting adjourned," said Charlotte and walked away.

18

Friday, 5:59 p.m.

I slipped into my place at the back of the table. I noticed something slimy ooze out of John Glenn's drawer and plop on the floor. I was an impartial observer for now, so I said nothing. But I did wonder how many germs might be growing in that slime.

Dad spooned the soup into bowls and handed them around the table. "Celery root is filled with plant nutrients and vital minerals," Dad explained. "Not to mention its dietary fiber."[45]

We began to eat. The chunks of pumpkin were not quite cooked long enough.

I took a deep breath and handed the bill from Mr. Grumpus to Dad. I figured I could wait until tomorrow morning to deal with John Glenn.

----

45   That is an important efficiency when you only have one working bathroom because . . . oh never mind.

I explained the bill.

"I see," said Dad.

I saw John Glenn out of the corner of my eye. He was pouring the soup into his drawer.

On top of the black beans, tacos, creamed spinach, and whatever else was in there. In went the soup.

The warmth of the soup was probably a perfect habitat for bacteria. I would have to check *Guide to Germs* after dinner.

"And if you didn't write in your book, who did?" Dad prompted.

I tried very hard not to look in Edison's direction. I also tried not to look at John Glenn. I am a scientist. I am an unbiased observer. I am not a tattletale. I could not tattle on Edison or John Glenn.

Just then Mom walked in. "What's that smell?" she asked.

It is possible to observe with your nose as well as your eyes. At least for Mom. Her nose is very well trained. I wondered about the smells coming from the bacteria growing in John Glenn's drawer.[46]

"Celery root and pumpkin stew," said Dad a little too proudly.

---

46   Some bacteria smell bad. This is how our primitive ancestors avoided eating rotten food.

"No. It smells funny," said Mom. "Like an old sock in a litter box in a musty basement."

Charlotte glanced primly in John Glenn's direction. Then she looked at me. Dad was talking about the second course. It was fish tartare with braised brussels sprouts.[47]

Mom noticed Charlotte's glance. I might as well give up on my hypothesis. Charlotte seemed to get all Mom's attention too. But then Mom looked at John Glenn and asked, "When was the last time you had a bath?"

So finally, Mom was paying attention to John Glenn. And finally I had some evidence to support my hypothesis.

---

47   Two very odiferous (or stinky) foods. Brussels sprouts are Barbie-sized cabbages. Fish tartare is raw fish blended with spices. Their smells are not from bacteria.

19

Friday, 7:32 p.m.

On Friday nights, Mom doesn't read her classics. She reads a picture book. She likes to get the boys to bed early. That's so she and Dad can have date night. It isn't really date night, because they don't go out. They usually don't go any farther than the back porch.

Tonight Mom was reading *Bartholomew and the Oobleck*. I have heard that story a hundred times, but I stayed long enough to hear about the greenish blobs of slime.[48]

After the greenish blobs started falling from the sky, I went to my room. Charlotte, Emily, and Anne were down in the rumpus room, so I had the place to myself.[49]

---

48   *Bartholomew and the Oobleck* is a book by Dr. Seuss. It is a book about a king who wants it to rain slime. And it does.

49   The rumpus room is just a fancy name for our family room. It is an ordinary family room. Mom just likes to use unusual words for ordinary things. Well, it is ordinary except for the chandelier and shag carpeting.

I walked over to Charlotte's dresser. I opened the Secret Notebook and looked at Anne's notes from the last SSS meeting.

If you want to read what she wrote, you'd better go get your dictionary. I'm serious!

Secret Notbook of the SSS

Date: September 10

Time: 3:49 pm., in the Year of the Dragon of McCarthian

Present: Queen Charlotte, Emily the Eccentric, and the Kind and Gracious Anne, the most beautiful princess in all the land, and Curious the Curious.

Meeting notes: The meeting was called to order by Queen Charlotte. She stood regally before her throne. A declaration was made, though not spoken aloud, that Emily the Eccentric would no longer be taking notes in the highly top secret notebook of the SSS. Queen Charlotte made a decree that the highly sought-after harmony of the McCarthy clan may plunge deeply into mass chaos.

Really. Read this Secret Notebook at your own risk. Unless you are at least twelve years old and at least in sixth grade. Otherwise, you'd better just skip to the next chapter.

The wayward pirate John Glenn has taken to disposing of our feast of questionable origin into the dungeons beneath the Magical Table and into Never Never Land.

It is evermore decreed that our secret agent, Curious the Curious, shall declare allegiance with the SSS. And upon declaring that allegiance, Curious the Curious will travel to distant lands and report John Glenn's swashbuckling behavior to the highly respected King and Queen-mother of McCarthian. She shall restore peace and harmony to the land evermore. Henceforth, Curious the Curious can continue her scientific quest until she is bestowed the Medallion of Science.[50]
Respectfully submitted: Anne Penelope Persephone Pandora Priscilla McCarthy

----

50   You aren't reading this, are you? Well that must mean you are at least twelve. So you probably figured out that this means Anne thought I might be a great scientist someday!

20

Saturday, 7:00 a.m.

I woke early. When I walked down the hall, I noticed that John Glenn was already up.

I walked downstairs to watch Dad make breakfast. I like to observe his efficient methods. And since I finally had a little success as a scientist — Mom had finally noticed John Glenn — I wanted to see if Dad would notice him too.

But I was out of luck. I didn't see John Glenn anywhere.

Dad was at the counter.

"Hi," I said.

"Hi, Curious," said Dad. "Do you want to help me scramble the eggs?"

"Okay."

Dad pulled out several spatulas. He picked out the perfect one and handed it to me.

I dragged the spatula across the hot pan.

I observed as the liquid eggs turned solid.

"The proteins in the eggs are changing their structure," said Dad. "It starts as a liquid. Then it turns into a solid."

He started to put things away. I thought I saw a hammer in the handful of spatulas he was putting in a drawer. That didn't seem to make sense. Hammers belong in his workshop. Dad is usually so organized.

I made a mental note of that observation and continued to scramble the eggs. The heat was causing the eggs to turn solid, but what had made the hot dog in John Glenn's drawer turn solid? The hot dog just sat there. But the eggs needed heat and a cook.

I wondered if there wasn't more than one way to be a scientist. Some scientists study and observe things — like paleontologists who look at fossils. But other scientists perform experiments — like chemists who add different things together to make new chemicals.

When I was done with the eggs, I slid behind the table. I was going to see what I could do about the petrified food problem.

Mom came in. "Good morning, Curious," she said.

"Hi," I said. She started reading the newspaper. Dad sat down and grabbed a section of the paper too. I thought that I might take advantage of their reading. Maybe I could quickly clean up the black bean-taco-carrot-creamed spinach mess. Then Charlotte wouldn't be mad at me.

Maybe I could be like a chemist and treat the drawer with hand sanitizer. That would prevent bacteria from growing on the nasty food. I could be a scientist who does more than observe.

But I didn't move quickly enough.[51]

The rest of the crew was coming down for breakfast. As they shoved and pushed and tumbled down the stairs, Anne asked, "Why did the man put scrambled eggs on his head?"

----

51   Remember, I am no Olympian.

We just stared at her. Anne is too cheerful in the morning.

"Because the hard-boiled ones kept falling off!" Anne laughed.

"Did he put bacon on his head too?" Ben asked seriously. Anne gave Ben a little shove. Ben fell and bumped into John Glenn, who had just come in from the living room. John Glenn reached past Ben and yanked on Anne's hair. Anne knocked into Emily, who was reading a book and not paying attention. Emily fell onto the floor at the bottom of the stairs.[52]

Mom and Dad ignored the battle. They were in their Saturday-morning-calm state.

Dad put out bacon, toast, and coffee. Then he put out the scrambled eggs. He looked at me and winked.

Mom grabbed her giant coffee mug and joined us at the table. Her mug said:

---

52   By now, you've figured out that this is another chain reaction.

My weekend is all BOOKED!

Dad grabbed his mug. It said:

ENGINEERS KNOW THE FORMULA FOR SUCCESS!

I watched as Dad picked up his fork. He pierced a small piece of bacon, a bit of scrambled egg, and a perfect square of toast. He popped these into his mouth and washed it down with a slurp of black coffee.

Breakfast was delicious. But John Glenn does not like eggs. He reached for his drawer and tried to slide it open. I saw his panic when he found the drawer nailed shut.

Dad smiled.

Charlotte dabbed her chin with her napkin. I saw scrambled eggs slither from beneath her napkin into her drawer.

I guess she does not like eggs either.

Original hypothesis: John Glenn would get noticed before Charlotte.

New hypothesis: John Glenn would get noticed eventually.

As a scientist, I felt good about getting my second hypothesis right. My life began in the fourth grade . . . with a new school and a new career.[53]

Conclusions

So how do you become a scientist? Trial and error. Science is not always about getting the hypothesis right the first time. Science is about being curious and making observations.

But science is about more than that. Science is about solving problems. And I might not have solved all my problems this week, but I have more weeks in fourth grade for that.[54]

After this week, I consider myself a *real* scientist.

Do you want to know something else about scientists? Scientists like to make conclusions.

----

53   As a scientist, in case you haven't figured that out already. A scientist is a person who studies one of the sciences. But you should know that, since this is Chapter 20. The only problem left is which kind of scientist will I be?
54   Someday I will figure out how to get out of the Green Group. Or why a school in a flat town is called Hilltop.

My conclusions are:

- Boundaries are for school districts and rabbits, not scientists.
- Teachers like books as much as they hate germs.
- Scientists need to use tissues to avoid being noticed.
- New schools and large families are good sources of bacteria.
- Imagination is not just for Fiction Week. It is for scientists too.
- And finally, scientists sometimes make predictions.[55]

I predict that Queen Charlotte will not kick me out of the Secret Sister Society for two reasons. First, she is going to need me to take notes. Second, I have some dirt on her — and she knows it.

---

55   Predictions are like forecasts. And just like the local meteorologist's, my forecast should be taken with caution.

SCIENCE STUNT
RECIPE FOR GREEN SLIME (or Oobleck!)

Mrs. Stickler wouldn't want you to make this, but she's not in charge of this book. You can also call this slime "Oobleck." Go ahead and say, "OOOOOO-BLECK!" It's fun. That's what they call the slime that falls from the sky in *Bartholomew and the Oobleck*. And you would know that if you had read the whole book and not just turned to the back.

What you need:

- a large bowl
- a measuring cup
- water
- cornstarch
- green food coloring

What you do:

1. Put 1 cup of water in the bowl.
2. Add 1½–2 cups of cornstarch to the bowl.
3. Mix with your hands.
4. Add the green food coloring.[56]
5. Play with it.

Oobleck has properties of both a liquid and a solid. Scientists call this a non-Newtonian fluid. Kids call it OOOOOO-BLECK!

---

56   Or you can add one drop of blue and one drop of yellow. That makes green. And you probably know that because only the smartest kids read all the way to the end of the book.

GLOSSARY

bacteria (bak-TEER-ee-uh) – single-celled microscopic creatures that exist everywhere in nature

biologist (by-AH-luh-jist) – a scientist who studies living things

coincidence (koh-IN-si-duhns) – something that happens accidentally at the same time as something else

declaration (dek-luh-RAY-shuhn) – an important announcement

dendrologist (den-DROL-uh-jist) – a scientist who studies trees

dovetail joint (DUHV-tayl JOINT) – a joint between two pieces of wood shaped like a dove's tail that form a wedge-shaped part that sticks out from one piece fitting tightly into a wedge-shaped slot in the other piece

eccentric (ek-SEN-trik) – different than what is accepted as normal; odd

efficient (uh-FISH-uhnt) – capable of getting things done without wasting time or energy

fungi (FUHN-jye) – organisms that have no leaves, flowers, or roots; mushrooms and molds are fungi

habitat (HAB-uh-tat) – the natural place and conditions in which a plant or animal lives

hypothesis (hye-POTH-uh-siss) – a prediction that can be tested about how a scientific investigation or experiment will turn out

minutes (MIN-its) – written notes that tell what took place at a meeting

observation (ob-zur-VAY-shuhn) – something that you have noticed by watching carefully

paleontologist (pay-lee-uhn-TAH-luh-jist) – a scientist who studies fossils

petrified (PET-ruh-fide) – a material that has been changed into stone or a stony substance by water and minerals

precise (pre-SISE) – very accurate or exact

FURTHER INQUIRIES

1. Curious made a hypothesis about John Glenn and Charlotte at dinner. Her first hypothesis wasn't right, but what happened with her second hypothesis?

2. Some of Curious's hypotheses came true and others didn't. What important step did Curious take to test her hypotheses?

3. Could reading help Curious be a better scientist? How?

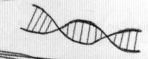

RECORD YOUR FINDINGS

1. Curious didn't tattle on John Glenn or Edison. Imagine she had tattled, and write a hypothesis on what would have happened.

2. Pretend you are a member of the SSS and it is your turn to take notes. Choose one of the meetings and write down what happened in your own words.

3. Choose one of the McCarthy children and write a hypothesis about what their favorite book or television show might be. Use details from the book to support your answer.

REFERENCES

A scientist should tell a reader where she got her information. We call these "References." Scientists do this in case the reader wants to do more research on the subject.

MRS. MCCARTHY'S AND
MRS. STICKLER'S REFERENCE LIST

Little House on the Prairie by Laura Ingalls Wilder

Treasure Island by Robert Louis Stevenson

Oliver Twist by Charles Dickens[57]

Charlie and the Chocolate Factory by Roald Dahl

Harry and the Horrible Slime by Suzy Kline

Bartholomew and the Oobleck by Dr. Seuss

Green Eggs and Ham by Dr. Seuss

The Snotty Book of Snot by Connie Colwell Miller

---

57   Don't try reading this yourself, unless you are a grown-up. And if you are a grown-up, you should read it to a kid.

ABOUT THE AUTHOR

Tory Christie is a real scientist by day and secretly writes children's books at night. When it is light outside, she studies rocks and water. After dark, she writes silly science stories that kids and grown-ups can laugh about. Although she grew up in a large family, her family was nothing like the McCarthys — honestly. The McCarthys are completely fictional — really. Tory Christie lives in Fargo, North Dakota, with her medium-sized family.

ABOUT THE ILLUSTRATOR

As a professional illustrator and designer, Mina Price has a particular love for book illustration and character design, or basically any project that allows her to draw interesting people in cool outfits. Mina graduated from the Maryland Institute College of Art with a BFA in Illustration. When she is not drawing, Mina can frequently be found baking things with lots of sugar or getting way too emotional over a good book.

MAKE MORE DISCOVERIES WITH CURIOUS!

FIND:

Videos & Contest
Games & Puzzles
Heroes & Villains
Authors & Illustrators

www.CAPSTONEKIDS.com

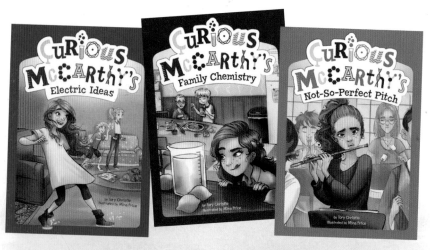